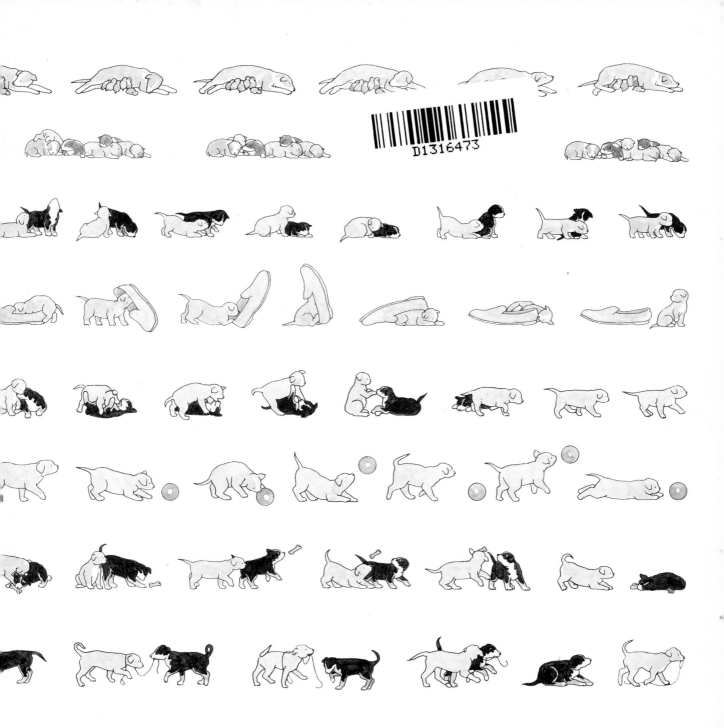

CREATED BY DORLING KINDERSLEY

Copyright © 1991 Dorling Kindersley Limited, London

All rights reserved.

Library of Congress Cataloging-in-Publication Data

Burton, Jane
  Puppy/photographed by Jane Burton.—1st American ed.
    p. cm.—(See how they grow)
  Summary: Photographs and text depict the growth and development of a
puppy from its first day alive to its eighth week.
  ISBN 0–525–67342–3
  1. Puppies—Juvenile literature. 2. Dogs—Development—Juvenile
literature. [1. Dogs. 2. Animals—Infancy.] I. Title.
II. Series.
SF426.5.B873 1991
636.7'07—dc20

                                                                    90–43262
                                                                         CIP
                                                                          AC

First published in the United States in 1991 by Lodestar Books,
an affiliate of Dutton Children's Books, a division of
Penguin Books USA Inc.

Originally published in Great Britain in 1991 by
Dorling Kindersley Limited, 9 Henrietta Street, London WC2E 8PS

Printed in Italy by L.E.G.O.   ISBN 0–525–67345–3
First American Edition   10 9 8 7 6 5 4 3 2 1

Written and edited by Angela Royston
Art Editor Nigel Hazle
Illustrator Rowan Clifford
Jane Burton was assisted by Hazel Taylor

Typesetting by Goodfellow & Egan
Color reproduction by Scantrans, Singapore

SEE HOW THEY GROW

PUPPY

photographed by
JANE BURTON

Lodestar Books • Dutton • New York

Just born

I am one day old.
I cannot see
or hear, but I
can smell.

I smell my mother
and crawl to her.
Now I am
sucking her
warm milk.

This is me

Asleep in a heap

I am nine days old.
I sleep snuggled up warm
and close to my
brothers and
sisters.

I open my eyes,
but everything is
a blur. I soon fall
asleep again.

Feeding time

I am two weeks old.
I am dreaming of milk,
and I whimper and sniff.

I wake up. Where is everyone? Oh no! They are feeding already.

I climb over Mom and push in too.

Exploring

I am three weeks old,
and I am growing fast.
I can see and hear and
walk very well.

Off I go to explore on my own.

Everything I find is new and interesting.

Playing with Dad

I am four weeks old, and I have my own bowl of food. Dad is licking it clean.

Come on, Dad.
Play with me.

Oh good, now
he is ready
to play.

Play fights

I am six weeks old
and much bigger
now. I love to play
with my toy rabbit.

My sister wants
to play with me.

But she has sharp
teeth, so I push
her away.

She is going off with my rabbit!

Ready to go

I am eight weeks old,
and I am wearing
my new collar
and leash.

My sisters are playing tug-of-war with their leashes.

My brother is trying to take me for a walk, but I don't want to go.

See how I grew

One day old

Nine days old

Two weeks old

Three weeks old

Four weeks old

Six weeks old

Eight weeks old

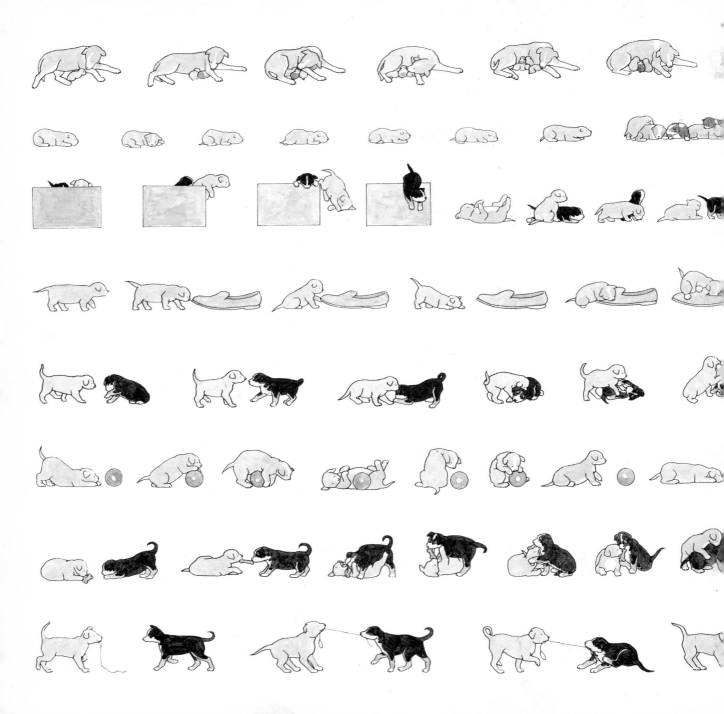